Eggs from the Chicken to You!

Heather Hammonds

Chapter 1	Eggs	2
Chapter 2	First Comes the Chicken	4
Chapter 3	At the Hatchery	6
Chapter 4	Egg Farms	10
Chapter 5	A Day in the Life of Henrietta	16
Chapter 6	After the Farm	18
Chapter 7	Follow the Egg Trail	22
Glossary and Index		24

Chapter 1 Eggs

Eggs are a very good food.
We eat them in lots of different ways.

The **vitamins** and **minerals** inside eggs help us to work, play and grow.

Most eggs we eat come from chickens. Some eggs come from other birds too.

quail

duck

chicken

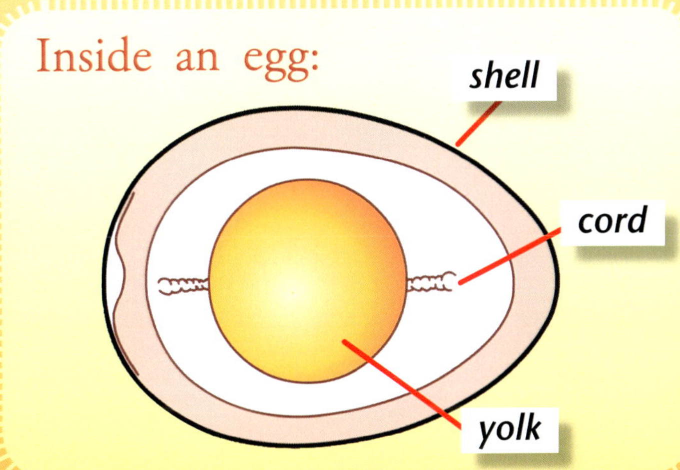

Chapter 2

First Comes the Chicken

Long ago there were only a few kinds of chickens. Today there are many different chickens.

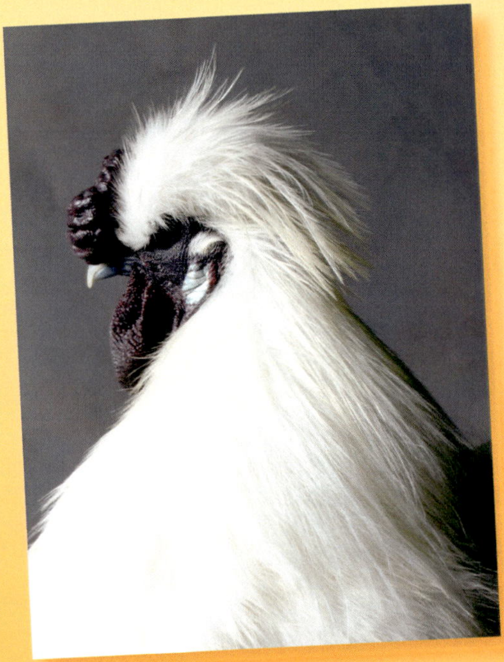

This chicken has lots of fluffy feathers.

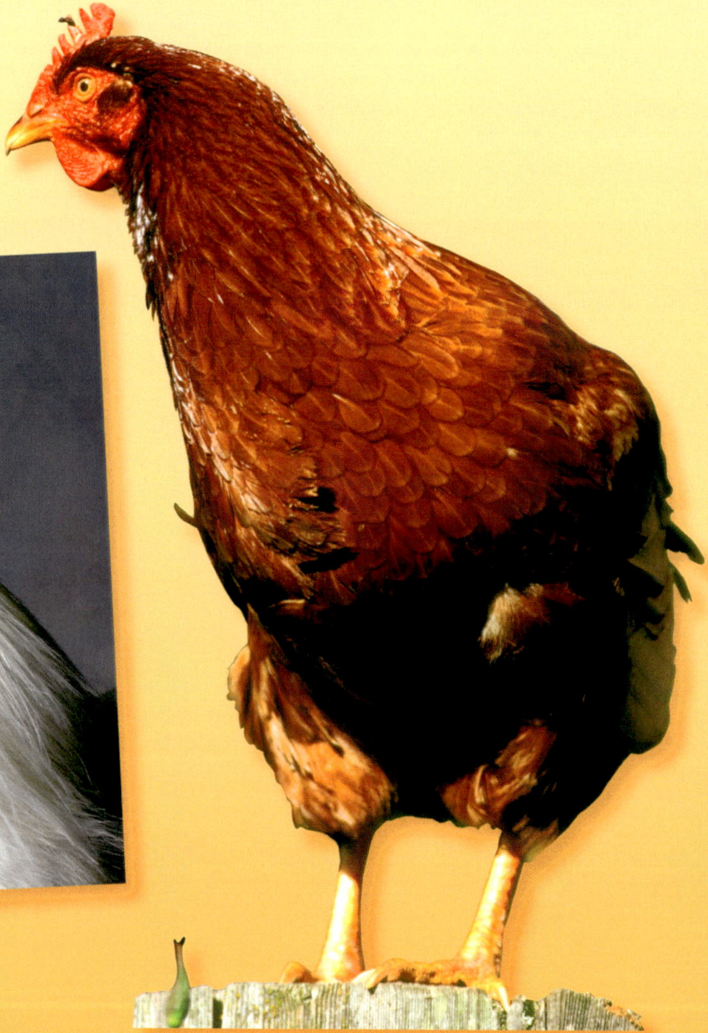

This chicken lays lots of eggs for us to eat.

Today most chickens are kept on big farms.

Some people keep chickens in their gardens too.

A male chicken is called a rooster. A female chicken is called a hen. Only hens lay eggs.

Chapter 3 At the Hatchery

Baby chickens are called chicks.
Most chicks are hatched at a chicken hatchery before going to farms.

an incubator

At the hatchery, eggs are kept in **incubators**. The incubators keep the chicks warm and safe as they grow inside the eggs.

Sometimes hens hatch their own chicks. They sit on the eggs in a nest.

It takes 21 days for chicks to hatch.

Baby chicks are kept in **brooders**. The chicks stay warm and safe in the brooders.

Chicks only hatch from **fertile** eggs. Eggs we buy to eat cannot hatch.

Chicks grow very quickly.
Soon they have all their feathers.

Young hens are called **pullets.**
Pullets are sold to egg farms.

Chapter 4 Egg Farms

Most eggs we buy come from egg farms.

Thousands of hens are kept at egg farms. Each hen lays an egg almost every day.

At some egg farms, hens are kept in cages. Two or three hens share each cage.

Many hens lay more than 300 eggs a year!

Hen cages are kept in big sheds at egg farms. The sheds are warm in winter and cool in summer.

Each cage has food and water for the hens. There are big lights in the sheds too.

The hens lay eggs in their cages. Then the eggs roll onto a **conveyor belt** and are taken away.

Eggs from hens that live in cages are called cage eggs.

At some egg farms, hens are kept in big barns. Hens lay their eggs in nesting boxes.

Eggs from hens that live in barns are called barn laid eggs.

At some egg farms, hens can go outside. They sleep in a barn, but they can peck in the grass outside too.

Eggs from hens that can go outside are called free range eggs.

Chapter 5

A Day in the Life of Henrietta

Henrietta lives on a free range egg farm. She is five months old and has just started to lay eggs. This is her day!

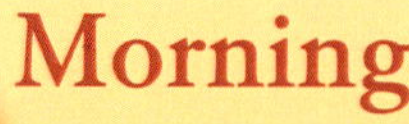

Morning

- wakes up

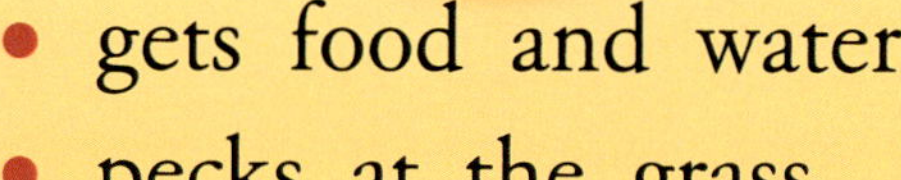

- gets food and water
- pecks at the grass

- goes outside

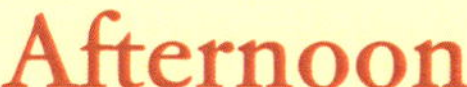

Afternoon

- goes inside
- LAYS EGGS!

- goes outside again
- gets more food and water

Night

- goes to sleep

Chapter 6 After the Farm

After eggs have been laid,
they are collected and kept in a **cool room**.

Then they are taken away from the egg farm.

Eggs from many farms are taken to big factories. The eggs are cleaned and special oil is sprayed on them, to keep them fresh.

The eggs are placed above a strong light, to check for cracks or marks inside them. This is called **candling** the eggs.

Next the eggs are stamped and sorted into different sizes. Then they are packed in cartons.

Trucks take the eggs to the shops, so we can buy them.

Each egg has a date stamped on it. This tells us how long our eggs will stay fresh.

Follow the Egg Trail

Follow the egg trail from the chicken to you!

1. It takes __ days for a chick to hatch.

3. Eggs from hens that can go outside are called __.

2. Young hens are called __.

Answers

1. 21
2. pullets
3. free range eggs

Glossary

brooders	machines that keep chicks warm and safe after they have hatched
candling	shining a very bright light on eggs to look inside them
conveyor belt	a machine with a long belt that takes eggs (and other things) from place to place
cool room	a very cold room that is like a large fridge
fertile	able to grow, or hatch
incubators	machines that keep eggs warm and safe while chicks inside them grow
minerals	small parts of food that are good for us
pullets	hens that are under one year old
vitamins	small parts of food that are good for us

Index

barn laid eggs 14
cage eggs 13
chicks 6–9, 22
egg farms 5, 6, 9, 10–15, 16–17, 18–19, 22–23
free range eggs 15, 16–17, 22
hens 5, 7, 9, 10–15, 16–17, 22, 23
pullets 9, 22–23
roosters 5